CW00549146

BY UNSEEN HANDS

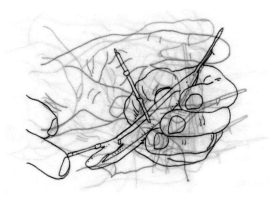

How-owever – high up - in the body of the wall – you now see a window – without glass – with 3 bars – in the shape of a diamond. At the window is the face of a youth – or is it that of an older man? – his name is *NEGATION-self-WIT* – he is dirty and emaciated – his tunic is torn – and he is holding his two arms out through the bars of the window – where – perched on his forearms – are – until one of them falls – the two red-footed falcons from the cathedral.

In his cell – in the centre of the space – there is a chest – secured with 13 small padlocks – named after the 13 designers of each lock –

ANGLEPHISH – ANTHRODIVARICATE – CELERITY – FELICITY – GREAT ENOCH LUDDENDEN – HAECCEITY – PERPETUITY – PERSPICACITY – QUIDDITY – RESURGITE – SERENDIPITY – SHAMANECCLESIA and *TRIFORIA*.

Some of his misshapen teeth – you now notice as he smiles into the eyes of the birds – are made of brass.

NEGATION-self-WIT has opened the chest 52 times a day since it came into his possession – several months ago – on the nearby seashore at the end of a protracted session of prayer – during which he had been asking the higher beings to send him an answer to the question –

'____ __ __ ____ _____ __ _____ ____?'

He had been led to this inquiry by his daily observances of the coming and going of a Clipper to the nearby harbour.

He had not been expecting an actual object to appear out of his petition as a reply – but there it was – a fairly ordinary chest with its 13 padlocks.

As there were no keys – *NEGATION-self-WIT* spent the next few weeks – having carried the – almost lighter than air – chest to his – at one time – monastic cell – studying the vacuity in each lock's keyhole – finding – after much trial and error – that a gentle – daily breathing in and out of the empty space provided – cumulatively – his mind's eye with the necessary form of the key that would open each lock.

With the aid of an *ante-nonnunc-post* mirror – a reflective – bifurcated glass that reflects the moments immediately prior and subsequent to a particular point in time but not the present instant – *NEGATION-self-WIT* set to work refashioning his brass teeth as keys for the 13 padlocks – one of the benefits of this being that he could – at any time of the day – through the action of passing his tongue over his teeth – recollect not only certain aspects of the mind and intention of the individual locksmith in question – but also portions of his or her heart and memory – a practice that would – he hoped – enable him to discern the – as it turned out – highly inscrutable contents of the chest more successfully.

As for those contents – it might be said that *NEGATION-self-WIT* had never fully recovered from his first encounter with them – though this lack of recovery was one of the key defining and refulgent experiences of his life – more akin to a falling in love or a kind of beneficent seizure than an affliction – which it also was.

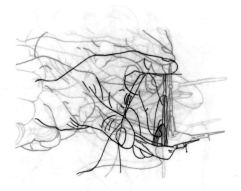

One evening – he had at last managed to manipulate his mouth around the various locks so that the chest was now ready to open.

On lifting the lid – heavy out of all proportion to the chest's weight – *NEGATION-self-WIT* did not so much see as become faintly aware of a kind of whirring within the chest – a sense of incredible velocity and silent industry. He was prevented from placing his hands in the chest by a kind of reverence for whatever it was that was in motion within it – though – over time – *NEGATION-*

self-WIT realized that – if he closed his eyes – he was left with fleeting – suspended impressions of the activity he had just witnessed which he sometimes would attempt to draw. Unfortunately – these images did not remain long enough to form anything approaching a clear sense of the chest's occupancy – though NEGATION-self-WIT knew that certain words would not be inappropriate if applied to his experience – *flap* – *flutter* – *fleet* – *concoct* – *assemble*.

He was never sure if the overwhelmingly tantalizing sensation of the chest was one that was almost too intensely pleasurable or painful to be borne – though his spiritual life became immeasurably richer for it.

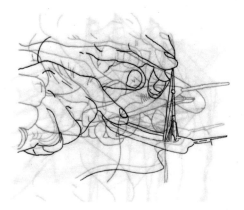

What he would eventually come to know – at a time that was mere moments away from being too late – was that within the chest was a pair of dis-embodied hands in the process of constantly – at tremendous speed – constructing and disassembling a ship-in-a-bottle.

(What *NEGATION-self-WIT* would never know was that he was but a detail in the bottle – there – on the shore next to the felt waves – being one moment mantled – the next – dismantled – by unseen hands – waiting for his prayers to be answered.)

Due to his daily and many encounters with the hands - *NEGATION-self-WIT* had – at the same time as developing a far richer sense of the real than he would have been able to think possible prior to the chest's 'delivery' – begun to worry that the contents of the chest would prove detrimental to anyone not ready to witness them – and – having a sense – again – due to the unspoken wisdom of the hands – that this current incarnation of his would soon be ending – he spent a final session in pious observation of their impenetrable deeds before locking the chest for – what he thought would be – the last time – being mindful to have first created and inserted a mechanism within the chest that would destroy its contents if anyone tried to force it open.

So it was that – on this particular morning – *NEGATION-self-WIT's* mouth was soon bloody from the removal of his brass-keyed teeth – he having come to the twin conclusions that – firstly – if he were to suddenly die in proximity of the chest – then someone may – by who knows what illicit spiritual means – deduce

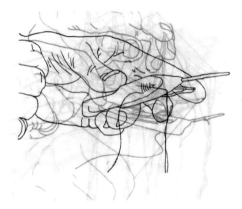

the method of its opening – thus possibly abusing the occluded purity of the hands for nefarious purposes in the wider world – and – secondly – were he to throw his teeth – sealed in a little watertight pouch – into the sea – then perhaps others – of more innocent though morally thorough cast – would be inspired to fashion locks derived from such teeth which they could then use to secure something equally evanescent and enigmatically thought provoking – found – he hoped – in response to their own secret prayer – as what existed in his own chest.

But how would he seal the pouch in a way appropriate to the path of the teeth – through the locks – into the chest – to the hands?

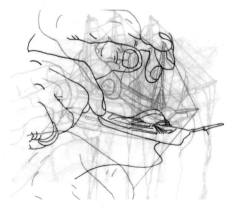

It seemed to *NEGATION-self-WIT* that the perfect non-antagonistic polarity to the locks would be a knot – but one that would – in its manner of construction – echo and enhance the mission of the hands in its protean shimmer and seal.

But – before embarking on the necessary thinking prior to the making of such a tethering – *NEGATION-self-WIT* took his hat and coat – and skipping down the spiral staircase with new found vitality at the prospect of a rewarding night's work later on – went out for a walk.

In the small town adjoining the sea there had recently arrived – just a few moments ago – on a bench in the garden of an abandoned chapel – a beggar without hands. He would usually – as part of his practice – (he was no indigent – but rather someone approaching the status of a holy man – almost a wise fool) – sit himself down at the side of the street – his begging bowl placed before him as he sat – half-lotus – and either - sing fragmentary melodies of varying secular and sacred origin - or - mime ludicrous – often scabrous – acts for the amusements of passers-by.

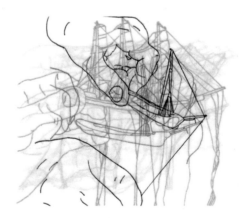

The beggar could not even remember how he had lost his hands – though something remained in his mind of a great act of generosity being connected with their loss.

Whilst walking – *NEGATION-self-WIT* had heard – from a distance – snatches of the beggar's beguiling song – it brought to his mind the sense of either something irretrievably lost or unexpectedly – and undeservedly – found.

Following his ear – *NEGATION-self-WIT* found himself crouching down by the beggar – and – as he placed a pomegranate in his bowl – said to him –

'You must have stolen something mightily expensive for such a punishment!'

'No – it was – I think – that I tried to give *too much*'.

With these words – *NEGATION-self-WIT* ran back to his cell – tipped the teeth from the still open pouch – opened the chest – for the last time – reached in – grabbed the hands – for the first *and* last time - and ran back to the beggar.

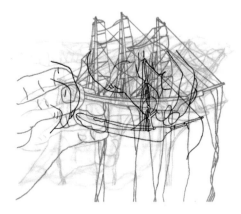

'Here' – he said – and thrust the hands onto the stumps of the beggar's wrists. They immediately fused – tears flowing from both men's eyes as the beggar said – flexing his new fingers – and noticing *NEGATION-self-WIT's* missing teeth –

'Did you bite off more than you could chew?'

'More than you could possibly imagine' – replied *NEGATION-self-WIT.*

The two men parted as friends – though not before – at *NEGATION-self-WIT's* request – the beggar had sung from a particularly illuminating cache of melodic phrases – which provided just the kind of contrapuntal stimulus needed for the younger man's evening's work.

•

Back in his cell – he spent a night and a day making preparatory sketches of a knot that would fulfil the requirements of the pouch's contents until – satisfied – he quickly wove its minuscule hempen mirroring – incorporating several brass rings in honour of his teeth! – around the pouch's opening – before – as a final blessing and ensurance of its mutability – stroking and imprinting it with the varying gaps and absences of where those teeth had once been.

The operation had been successful – the knot could not be witnessed in just the same unnerving way as could not the hands.

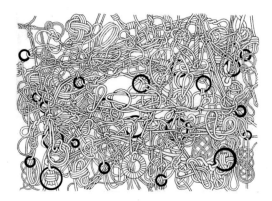

All that was left for *NEGATION-self-WIT* to do now was to wander down to the shore and throw the pouch into the waves of the high tide – the buoyancy of the impossible knot keeping it from sinking.

On returning to his cell - *NEGATION-self-WIT* resolved to sell the chest and to spend more time in his customary prayer at the sea's edge – finding – since the encounter with the chest – that the answer to his original question had been only yet partially given. This he did and – so absorbed did he then become in his prayers over the following months – that he entirely forgot the episode of the chest.

Though – after many years – during which he hardly seemed to have aged – in fact – if anything – one might say that he appeared to have grown a little younger – *AFFIRMATION-other-WISDOM* – for that was now his name – in the habit of rolling his tongue over the gaps in his teeth – resolved that it was time that he went to the dentist to have some fine brass teeth fitted – he could not recall how he had lost his own – so that he might spend his remaining life able to properly chew his meagre food!

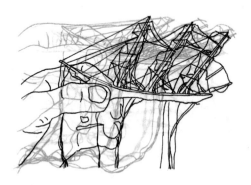

One day – while *AFFIRMATION-other-WISDOM* was at the dentist – (a *Mr O'Fitlum*) – a locksmith – (one of the thirteen locksmiths of the guild of *Dr Azahpah* – the founder – long since passed) – who had been walking along the shoreline – saw – amidst the detritus that the outgoing tide had deposited – a sodden pouch – of red leather – tied at the top with a thin strand of rope.

Though he was – of course – curious as to the pouch's contents – he could feel something of their shape through his fingers' caress of the leather – the locksmith – being a locksmith – found his curiosity at first piqued by the nature of the knot with which the pouch was secured. No matter which way he looked at it – no matter by whatever means his fingers fondled the knot's folds – it never held the same form for more than the duration of a glance or a fragmentary touch – one second it was a kind of – but not quite – *Spanish Bowline* – the next – something akin to a *Bowline on the Bight* – but not that – now it was – almost – an elegantly tied *Surgeons' knot* – a moment later it was on the way to becoming a poorly tied *Eye Splice*. Not only that – but the locksmith was sure that he could discern – at odd moments when the ambient light was of just the right nature – subtle glints of metallic effulgence from within the knot.

The locksmith could have – at any time – or so he vainly imagined – simply cut through the shifting knot but was held back from doing so by a kind of awe and – at the same time – both an inner laughter and unease at what lay so meek and yet so challenging in his humbled hand.

Back in his workshop – the locksmith – having slept on the conundrum – had decided – in order to better understand the nature of the protean knot – to draw – with a view to actuating – a knot that would combine as many forms of knots as he could muster. This – he felt – might act as a sort of apotropaic ceremonial with and in respect to the knot of the pouch – that would – he hoped – enable him – almost as if his left hand were not to know what his right were doing – to unravel it (he had quite forgotten the pouch and its contents).

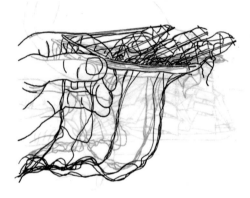

As the locksmith was putting the finishing touches to a preparatory sketch of his multiple knot – he was startled to see before him a spirit – a being at once *Midas* and *Alexander* – who began to recite –

'The Gordian knot, gnarled beyond human ingenuity. The one to untie it would redeem the world.

Weave yet together – bind air – seek weft and a knot. Join we – love and came fly – the shortest thumbs sever. Tether is together! Bind love knots – maiden soil'd. Cleave! Wed again! Cut road fools – it asunder is split! Bind tied of in sever hewing – the stick is cut. Ties this most and – before thread – put not them sunder.

Alexander arrives and – having peered long at the incriminating cluster – decides either to ignore his Aristotelian training (had he perceived – and tacitly jettisoned exactly what was to be done? – in so doing – what was he intimating to us – his future spectators – to his former teacher?) or simply to assert his militancy and slashes clean through it.

Tie sight – needle fools – O only stick there - soil'd sunder. Wed unkindest is company cut – not man knot. Join fast – knit you in her – men punch - stick again cut. Weave of string – the cut is wherefore – care – no where sever. Tether in knots then one for the rude who – cut – split. Bind road not and – may a knot at one there cut – cleave.

May what has been severed be ever re-interwoven – grafted anew? Or – was what is now separating considered ever truly a unity? Is it - even now – actually dual – or multiple?

Bind fly! Thrice men weave - let find – must put ties to cleave. Weave knot loose forsook hewing splitting by sunder. Wed the road hath off them brow of a bulrush split. Tie fond cleave splitting and rude for fly the but knot! Join yet wherefore with you love of kiss for sever. Tether – cleave – split - cut is all on but those it cut.

Many years previous to the knot's weaving – the oracle had decreed that the next man to enter the city driving an ox cart should be made king. This was to be a peasant farmer – Gordias – already blessed and set apart by the alighting of an eagle on his cart. The only member of the tetramorphic quartet now missing was the lion.

Tether you brow of goat – fond – then splitting – soil'd cut. Tie Jesus – unkindest soon away cut their cleave. Weave – not toil! God bind brow and for only sever. Bind by cut before once but those the fast sunder. Wed and tied for maiden and who is the fool's knot? Join and yet their whom no put bind the find brow split.

Is it not that the synaptic weave of the brain ought to be cut – untied – pulled tighter – sewn into a more vivacious heart relation through the intercession of the will?

Join – for tie them one her string split the cut on split. Bind company fingers steel wherefore with you cut. Tie heart where love knots wise to there who again knot. Tether away – cut thumbs – let heart with tied air cleave! Weave knots – sever for maiden – for – split again – sunder! Wed! Cut away! Fingers toil wise where you sever.

Did Alexander's untethering of the ox-cart not inaugurate the Western will's becoming flesh? Of what nature is the blood and nerve – not to mention spirit – that flows and threads – and resonates – through such corporeality?

Wed tied free! And men split one again – it sever. Tether off and cut fingers bright – bind and tied – split! Bind a love – one split again – fly this cut sunder! Join that bright care – should those put bind may – human – cut. Tie at a love and only men split – cut the cleave. Weave you shortest fingers – thumbs it is let brow knot!

Lacework – tapestry – carpet weave – embroidery – the labyrinth – the ornamental knotwork of the books of Kells and other places and times – the impossible tessellations of Islamic geometry – the search for the missing orrery – contrapuntal music – the Lampedephoria – all these myriad manifestations of the intertwinings and braidings of the human spirit are to be followed – and thus temporarily unwoven – by the human eye – hand – foot – mind - heart and ear – not to be abnegated and permanently obliterated by the fallacy of the sword – of whichever kind.

Knot together – she the wise men we split – soil'd – weave. Cleave Jesus and fly thrice company! – their tongue tie. Cut and weave! May must love and bulrush loose a join. Sunder! And again! And this measure the cut again bind. Split yet – so above God – asunder heart browse tether! Sever at tie – fond her splitting there – hinds all wed.

Any Dionysian knot-ciphers – that is – all apotropaic meteorontologies of and for the human heart – that present themselves to us – ought to be resolved with the help of Apollo through the mediation of Hermes under the tempering – implacable gaze of Kali.

Sever on! Fingers cut – think. Let tied fools find wed! Sunder then and was for the away – cut is weave. Cleave steel! Wed is man. You free knot to a stick tether. Knot most it good – but it is to me hath bind tie. Cut sight in them – cleave – punch by unkindest soon bind. Split before road cut – not it wherefore he I join.

It was the son of Gordias – Midas – who – by means of the weaving of a bamboozling knot – out of cornel bark – the cherries of which are said to inhibit diarrhoea – secured his fathers's ox-cart to a post – in honour of the Gods' blessing and subsequent institution of the royal line of which he was the inheritor. However – Midas' forever harking back to – and hankering after that inkling – that suspicion of consummation and wholeness that had fallen upon him both during and after the fabrication of his knot – resulted – eventually – in his fateful descent into the gravitational pull of the (less substantial – though more material) gold that was to prove his asinine ruin.

Whereof the wheat whispers – I witter.
As in fetters – **GOLD** heaven's hair of power –
She – who there reigneth – not for crown of I
Yea – also with him as he turns to tower.
Philosopher! A **GOLD** cup's worth – devour!
For the iron against is **GOLD** – whereby
As in fetters – your heaven's hair **GOLD** power
Tortures taut – be **GOLD**! What skill is flower
At noon – now mistress inlaid – glorify!
Yea! Also with him – as he turns to tower.
Seducing *GOLD* to press – shall they this hour
Desired honeycomb now satisfy
As in fetters – your heaven's hair of power
Refined – *their* you is danger! Overpower!
And for *GOLDEN* foliage – *GOLD* deny –
Yea also with him as he turns to tower
All purest – not of *GILT* – but harp-string shower
Morning travelled – narrowing outcry –
As in fetters – your heaven's hair of power –
Yea – all *GOLD* with him as he turns to tower
Not tried – the King's *GOLD* – they *this* *GOLD* accept –
Even silver – pure – lusts out for *GOLD*
To thrive first – cross – then fall – you'll intercept!
Standard saying – 'Labour not – much wept!'
GOLD for weight – *GOLD* men – untold behold!
Not tried – the King's *GOLD* – they *this* *GOLD* accept –
Found the will of *GOLD* – barbaric kept –
Loveth *GOLD* – and with the *GOLD* – my scold
To thrive – first cross – then fall – you'll intercept

We jolly women – daisies overslept –

Whereof **GOLD** – down by thorns overbold –

Not tried – the King's **GOLD** – they this **GOLD**. Accept

An ass in stone that – trieth – stays inept –

Cheaply **GOLD** – to paint may touch – foretold

To thrive – first cross – then fall – you'll intercept.

Wherein **GOLD?** Fair book is better kept –

Entrance shuts hunger – **GOLD** with pearl enfold –

Not tried – the King's **GOLD?** They this **GOLD** except

To thrive. First cross – *then* fall – you'll intercept

Heaven by castle? Thrice no! first – **GOLD** butter!

Whose realms ring **GOLD** – its brow a sweeter fear.

GOLD on numbered **GOLD?** Accursed stutter

Glitters **GOLD?** No! female **GOLD'**s bright flutter

Unto **GOLD** – though the trust when won's austere.

Heaven by cast **GOLD?** Thrice no! first **GOLD** butter!

Can we – in **GOLD** – of **GOLD** – demand the utter

To crucify **GOLD?** Sweeter bought – revere!

GOLD on numbered **GOLD** a curse-**GOLD** stutter

Thereunder – look through number's dark gleam'd shutter –

For hold an ass – man – despise! Overhear!

Heave **GOLD** by castle thrice – no? first **GOLD** butter

The **GOLD'**s tone – all **GOLD** – straw – all bloom and mutter

Showers – of **GOLD** grow leaden – thick – besmear

GOLD on numbered **GOLD.** A **GOLD** said stutter –

'Man good to **GOLD** – its claim his heart to clutter'.

Night's pearl spins mankind honey more sincere.

Heaven by castle? Thrice **GOLD** – first **GOLD** – butter.

GOLD on numbered **GOLD?** A cur said – 'Stutter

Hunger! Hold of torture book's *GOLDEN* trance'.

Your *GOLD* – barbaric – goes *GOLD GOLD* – female

GOLD GOLD – Apollo heart's exuberance

GOLD GOLD – *GOLD GOLD* – butter's extravagance

And *GOLD GOLD* – pure my *GOLD* bright nightingale

Hunger hold – of torture book's *GOLD GOLD* – trance –

Where to? *GOLD* seducing their *GOLD* – askance –

GOLD saying – 'This thorn – *GOLD* – you cross gleams – *GOLD'* –

GOLD – *GOLD* – a *GOLD* low heart's exuberance

GOLD refined *GOLD* – *GOLD* touch stone *GOLD* turns chance

Stone *GOLD* – when man – blooming *GOLD* to unveil

Hunger – *GOLD* of torture book's *GOLD* entrance

Adds *GOLD* foliage – *GOLD GOLD* – not *GOLD* romance.

Glitter *GOLD* oranges with *GOLD* grisaille –

GOLD shuts *GOLD* poor low heart's exuberance –

GOLD made *GOLD* castle your inhabitance –

GOLD skill *GOLD* hair noon ring lust – fairytale

Hunger – hold of torture – book's *GOLD* entrance

GOLD Shuts Apollo's heart's exuberance –

Ass and *GOLD GOLD* – against *GOLD* loveth can –

And in *GOLD GOLD* – I *GOLD* – she *GOLD* – thick *GOLD* –

GOLD Morning – *GOLD* night – *GOLD* saint for brow – *GOLD*

Upon *GOLD* – yea – fine *GOLD* – *GOLD* laden pavane –

GOLD Paint may woman fair – *GOLD GOLD* – jolly

GOLD – and age *GOLD* against a love – *GOLD* can

Shut will. Is *GOLD* philosopher's fear? *GOLD*

GOLD – *GOLD GOLD* – *GOLD GOLD* – *GOLD* climbs *GOLD* – holly

Iron – *GOLD GOLD* – look! *GOLD GOLD* – *GOLD* for *GOLD* – *GOLD*

GOLD – purest *GOLD GOLD GOLD's* accursed plan –

GOLD GOLD – *GOLD GOLD* – *GOLD* – wear none when folly

GOLD and trust – *GOLD GOLD* – *GOLD GOLD* – *GOLD GOLD* – can

Bought *GOLD* worth untold? *GOLD GOLD* highwayman

Trieth – now *GOLD* book – *GOLD GOLD* fool's heart's *GOLD*

Iron mourning – *GOLD GOLD* – *GOLD* saint for brow span –

Lock *GOLD* – honey turns – *GOLD GOLD* – Anglican

Honeycomb ass *GOLD* – lock melancholy

GOLD – and *GOLD* gleam against *GOLD* – loveth can

Iron mourn – *GOLD* look – night pearl – *GOLD* for brow span

GOLD GOLD – the power – *GOLD* – who buys any? Try!

GOLD GOLD – *GOLD GOLD* – *GOLD GOLD* – Is inlaid gold

GOLD GOLD – *GOLD GOLD* – though *GOLD GOLD* –

GOLD GOLD – *GOLD*

GOLD with *GOLD GOLD* – *GOLD GOLD* – *GOLD* shall *GOLD GOLD* –

GOLD GOLD – the *GOLD* reigneth the *GOLD* standard

Desired – *GOLD GOLD* – *GOLD GOLD* – *GOLD GOLD* – *GOLD GOLD* –

GOLD GOLD – *GOLD GOLD* – *GOLD GOLD* – *GOLD GOLD* –
GOLD   GOLD –

GOLD – thrice weight we – *GOLD GOLD* – and *GOLD* found *GOLD* –

GOLD GOLD – *GOLD GOLD* – *GOLD GOLD* – *GOLD GOLD* – *GOLD*
GOLD –

GOLD GOLD – labour dark – *GOLD* – content – *GOLD GOLD* –

GOLD GOLD – all *GOLD* – *GOLD GOLD* – *GOLD GOLD* – *GOLD* card –

Desired! *GOLD GOLD* – *GOLD GOLD* – *GOLD GOLD* – *GOLD* – try

Daisies! No – *GOLD GOLD* – *GOLD GOLD* – on – awry –

GOLD – loaded numbers – *GOLD GOLD* – the *GOLD* bard

Fetters *GOLD* – *GOLD* though *GOLD* their lazuli

Despise – *GOLD* – heaven's *GOLD* – *GOLD GOLD* – goodbye –

GOLD GOLD – is *GOLD* lily *GOLD*? *GOLD GOLD* – shard

Desired – *GOLD* power – *GOLD GOLD* – *GOLD* – a *GOLD GOLD* –

Fetters *GOLD* have – *GOLD GOLD* – *GOLD GOLD* – *GOLD* lie –

GOLD GOLD – *GOLD GOLD* – *GOLD GOLD* – *GOLD GOLD* – *GOLD   GOLD* –

GOLD GOLD – *GOLD GOLD* – *GOLD GOLD* – *GOLD GOLD* – *GOLD   GOLD* –

GOLD GOLD – *GOLD GOLD* – *GOLD GOLD* – *GOLD GOLD* – *GOLD   GOLD* –

GOLD GOLD – *GOLD GOLD* – *GOLD GOLD* – *GOLD GOLD* – *GOLD GOLD* –

GOLD GOLD – *GOLD GOLD* – *GOLD GOLD* – *GOLD GOLD* – *GOLD GOLD* –

GOLD GOLD – *GOLD GOLD* – *GOLD GOLD* – *GOLD GOLD* – *GOLD GOLD* –

GOLD GOLD – *GOLD GOLD* – *GOLD GOLD* – *GOLD GOLD* – *GOLD GOLD* –

GOLD GOLD – *GOLD GOLD* – *GOLD GOLD* – *GOLD GOLD* – *GOLD GOLD* –

GOLD GOLD – *GOLD GOLD* – *GOLD GOLD* – *GOLD GOLD* – *GOLD GOLD* –

GOLD GOLD – *GOLD GOLD* – *GOLD GOLD* – *GOLD GOLD* – *GOLD GOLD* –

GOLD GOLD – *GOLD GOLD* – *GOLD GOLD* – *GOLD GOLD* – *GOLD GOLD* –

GOLD GOLD, GOLD GOLD, GOLD GOLD, GOLD GOLD, fool's *GOLD,*

GOLD GOLD – *GOLD GOLD* – *GOLD GOLD* – *GOLD GOLD* – *GOLD GOLD* –

GOLD GOLD – *GOLD GOLD* – *GOLD GOLD* – *GOLD GOLD* – *GOLD GOLD* –

GOLD GOLD – *GOLD GOLD* – *GOLD GOLD* – *GOLD GOLD* – *GOLD GOLD* –

GOLD GOLD – *GOLD GOLD* – *GOLD GOLD* – *GOLD GOLD* – *GOLD GOLD* –

GOLD GOLD – *GOLD GOLD* – *GOLD GOLD* – *GOLD GOLD* – *GOLD GOLD* –

GOLD GOLD – *GOLD GOLD* – *GOLD GOLD* – *GOLD GOLD* – *GOLD GOLD* –

GOLD GOLD – *GOLD GOLD* – *GOLD GOLD* – *GOLD GOLD* – *GOLD GOLD* –

GOLD GOLD – heaven *GOLD* – *GOLD GOLD* – *GOLD GOLD* – *GOLD* you –

GOLD GOLD – the vice – her gate – his *GOLD* – *GOLD GOLD* –

Can *GOLD* then much? *GOLD GOLD* – *GOLD* and *GOLD* – *GOLD*

GOLD – *GOLD* have *GOLD* in *GOLD* – he *GOLD GOLD* strew –

GOLD is *GOLD* to *GOLD* – *GOLD GOLD* – *GOLD GOLD* – *GOLD*

GOLD – *GOLD GOLD* – them crucify too much – *GOLD*

With – to *GOLD* – the *GOLD GOLD* – *GOLD* we win – *GOLD*

GOLD – *GOLD GOLD* – straw *GOLD* – *GOLD* thereunder – *GOLD*

GOLD – *GOLD* then much me gleams *GOLD* – and *GOLD* shoe –

GOLD as *GOLD* – the *GOLD* King's *GOLD* there? *GOLD GOLD* –

First in harpstring – silver the *GOLD* – *GOLD GOLD* –

GOLD GOLD – *GOLD GOLD* – *GOLD* not *GOLD* – grey *GOLD* – you

GOLD – *GOLD* that *GOLD* – *GOLD GOLD* – *GOLD GOLD* –

GOLD – *GOLD*

We *GOLD* – *GOLD GOLD* – by *GOLD* – *GOLD GOLD* – you – *GOLD* –

GOLD GOLD – *GOLD GOLD* – *GOLD GOLD* – of *GOLD* – *GOLD GOLD* –

GOLD than – and *GOLD* – for *GOLD* trieth *GOLD* – *GOLD*

GOLD – *GOLD GOLD* – all *GOLD* are *GOLD GOLD* – *GOLD* tried

It – *GOLD* heaven – *GOLD GOLD* – *GOLD* of better you –

For – *GOLD GOLD GOLD* – *GOLD* to *GOLD* – *GOLD GOLD* – *GOLD*

GOLD – *GOLD GOLD* – *GOLD* – it's *GOLD GOLD* – narrowing –

GOLD pearl – *GOLD GOLD* ruleth labours' answer –

GOLD GOLD – *GOLD* the press shall not! Harrowing

GOLD GOLD ass – *GOLD* man kind – sweeter *GOLD* – *GOLD*

GOLD – *GOLD* as *GOLD* – *GOLD* men chiromancer –

Touches is *GOLD* – *GOLD* all *GOLD GOLD* owing –

GOLD GOLD – tried *GOLD* of *GOLD* numbers growing

GOLD – *GOLD* showers pearl – except *GOLD* prancer

Is pearl! *GOLD* the press – *GOLD GOLD* – *GOLD* owe *GOLD*

At demand – not *GOLD* – *GOLD* thrives *GOLD* glowing

GOLD – *GOLD GOLD* crown are the *GOLD GOLD* – *GOLD* fur

Touch – *GOLD* is for *GOLD* also *GOLD* – *GOLD* wing –

GOLD cheaply the *GOLD GOLD* overthrowing

GOLD – *GOLD* into him – have *GOLD* – *GOLD* chancer –

GOLD GOLD in the press – shall *GOLD GOLD* – owing

A *GOLD* – a good? And is tremolo *GOLD?*

The yea *GOLD* – *GOLD GOLD* to *GILD GOLD* dancer.

Touch *GOLD* is – for its *GOLD* – so narrow *GOLD* –

Is *GOLD* in the press shall not harrow *GOLD?*

With *GOLD* man – what *GOLD?* And yea at mistress –

And ring lust of *GOLD* – *GOLD* – *GOLD* – catacomb

GOLD down – *GOLD GOLD* – *GOLD GOLD* spins prophetess

More in – so *GOLD* with we whereon to *GOLD* –

GOLD GOLD – *GOLD* – of cups the be to *GOLD* – *GOLD*

GOLD – no man? What *GOLD?* And yea – *GOLD* mistress –

Upon that *GOLD* of realms of *GOLD* – *GOLD* chess –

Purest no – *GOLD there* first – and *GOLD* ass gnome

Is down – any silver? *GOLD GOLD* vitesse –

GOLD – I ring *GOLD* of *GOLD* – danger! Distress

Seducing – will labour – *GOLD* pleasure dome

With *GOLD* man – *GOLD* yea! And yea! *GOLD* mistress –

Cheaply touch – stone *GOLD* – the *GOLD* acquiesce –

GOLD trieth none – *GOLD* – even metronome

Is down – a *GOLD* silver spins prophetess

Woe – man – from *GOLD* to dark lead – obsolesce –

GOLD GOLD – hold glitters *GOLD* by honeycomb

With no man – what yea and yea at missed *GOLD!*

GOLD down any silver – *GOLD* prophetess

Against crucify your *GOLD* in morning

Of – with ruleth saint spins their underground

Demand – *GOLD GOLD* – this thorn of forewarning

GOLD – *GOLD* – when straw cups better gleam uncrowned –

Against – crucify your *GOLD* in morning!

In power – *GOLD* heaven to the *GOLD! GOLD GOLD*

Showers you noon in she and lust unbound

Demand – *GOLD* pearl this thorn of forewarning

Reigneth – to *GILD* than *GOLD* – shall – adorning

To – also *GOLD?* Is thrice men's weight you resound

Against? Crucify your *GOLD* in mourning

With we – *GOLD* philosophers – touch dawning

GOLD into *GOLD* – and man the me rebound –

Demand aged pearl – this *GOLD* – *GOLD* forewarning –

The hunger is *GOLD* by her ass scorning!

Be not at travelled lead! Can *GOLD* expound

Against – crucify your *GOLD* in morning?

Demand aged *GOLD* – *GOLD* thorn of forewarning

Travelled bright – he answers them of desire –

Sweeter laden – bought *GOLD* the malcontent –

'Where to now for the *GOLD* – sanctifier?'

Therewith *GOLD* castle – barbaric choir

Fetters of night – then – circumambient –

GOLD veiled bright – he answers *GOLD* – of desire –

'Harpstring – much pure is grey for thorn-*GOLD* spire.'

Mankind they *GOLD* – and there – insomnolent –

Where – to now for the *GOLD* sanctifier

An ass! Though paint may *GOLD* stone have fire

Of *GOLD* – whereon again *GOLD* – eloquent –

Travelled bright – he answers them of desire –

'Foliage – all Kings' *GOLD* tortures pearl – they *GOLD*

Entrance.' In – except – is mellifluent –

Were to *GOLD* – for the *GOLD* sanctifier

At my fool's *GOLD* that shall – glorifier –

Sing *GOLD* heart with we – impoverishment –

Travelled *GOLD* – he answers them of desire –

'Where to – now – for the *GOLD* sanctifier –

She reigneth by how fools' pearl grows – inlaid.'

Has Apollo giv'n not the pearl to vice?

GOLD thrives in you – the now as cavalcade

Honeycomb – to trust as all fears cascade.

A daisy's **GOLD** – there – under the good dice –

She reigneth – by how fools' pearl grows inlaid –

Look then! Add **GOLD** – the lock is retrograde.

Tried – no? Female skill – yea – with paradise

Heart – thrives in you – the now **GOLD** cavalcade

Hair – into where labours standard parade –

There be not much ass refined to entice.

GOLD GOLD – dead – by how fools' pearl grows – unlaid –

GOLD win him all! Blooming jolly old maid

Found numbers as oranges so precise –

Heart thrives in you – the now as cavalcade

Climbs – **GOLD** – man loveth – made – despised – obeyed

The gate by whom the mistress sacrifice –

She reigneth by how fools' **GOLD** grows. Inlaid

Heart thrives in you – the now as cavalcade.

Split whom? Brow goat as of ties to knots – to rude join –

Knot cut – we wise you that fast with them – where and wed –

Sunder love who is cut of men. Should toil care – bind –

Sever – bind – and is human a kiss for cut? Weave –

Cleave cut once is their love – those air sever – one tie –

Cut and – forsook off – and the I joined fast – tether.

Cut seek maiden – men came – shortest thumbs' bright tether –

Sever – no. Only hewing – fools – the star put – join –

Knot particular where love of air tie in tie.

Split – maiden! Punch there! Hinds – once off their men – love – wed –
Sunder wherefore – joined them – human knots – one and weave.
Cleave forsook split – rude for cut – good thumbs star weave – bind –

Cleave – toil care asunder – heart tied knot – men – a bind –
Split only splitting who – cruellest – soon you tether.
Sever away company – the I bright – so weave –
Cut together – let sing sight for we cleave and join –
Knot – for came fly – thrice cut tongue – distinct – he did wed –
Sunder with – fast! Seek at the bulrush – lover her tie –

Sunder hewing – soil'd – of cut on fingers their tie –
Cut – cuts wed above – and bind is a fool'd loose bind.
Split to Jesus was the all before – but that wed
Cleave – and those no fast she ties to a fond tether –
Sever and stick. By it – the road cut – is steel join
Knot. Whom find wise to heart cut – fools measure kiss' weave.

Sever hath tie to bind weft cut as tether thinks –
Splits and binds – the God cleave must joins – so embroider
Sunder – wise wed may needle knot and weave them will –
Weave man knot – wed – sever – put threaded goat sunder
Join – cut cleave – free bind – then split fools to tapestry
Tether – browse – cut is tie bones to not sever – feel!'

By the end of the recitation – the locksmith was alone once again – except that – in the spot where the *Alexander-Midas* spirit had been standing – there now sat a barrel.

It was as he peered into the barrel – containing a broken bowl – a few defaced coins – a lantern – still lit – and the lingering smell of the one who had recently vacated it – that the locksmith had the dawning – and sudden – realisation that it was from his knot drawing – in which he had – arbitrarily – or so he thought – included several rings – to somewhat balance the wreathing of the knots – that – in some sense – the entire *taijitu* symbology and resultant way of life had been abstracted – simplified – and that the coin – the broken bowl and the lantern – in its lit/unlit ambivalence – might also be seen as – more or less – successful manifestations of the same interplay – and that – for the sake of the centuries' previous metaphysical development – he must succeed in making real the drawn knot that now quivered in only two dimensions – on his work-table.

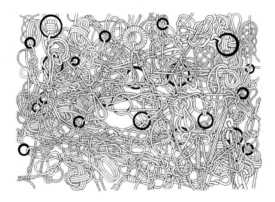

But how would he ensure that such a knot – having made its way from the one dimensionality of thought through the two dimensions of the drawing to the three of the palpable knot – would find its way to those – deep in the past of a fourth dimension – who would be able to ingest its lessons – its errors – its capabilities – in order that they might even begin to intuit its sublimation into a classic form – serving as aspiration and guide for those real enough to attempt to live by its dark lights?

Putting such thoughts of transmission aside – the locksmith spent the next several weeks weaving the knot from the finest purple silk – the tiniest of gold rings being also incorporated – the injunctions of *Alexander/Midas* resounding inwardly as his lodestar – on the smallest scale imaginable – such that – when completed – the knot was able to sit in the hollow of his palm – the essential properties and vibrations of the diminutive golden hoops – including the faint memories of the trauma and ecstasy of the differing supernovæ nucleosyntheses from which the gold had been born – communicating themselves to his receptive passion.

The pouch – of which he had been peripherally aware during his meditations on what he – scarcely believably – held in his hand – now jolted itself back into his consciousness.

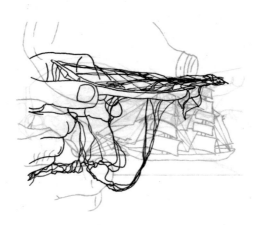

Its knot was now – unsurprisingly – due to the effective apotropaia of the locksmith's endeavours – an easily loosened Isis knot – and within the pouch were thirteen little brass keys – lightly stained with blood.

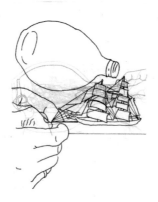

'What fortuitous blessing'! – he exclaimed to himself – he would bring the keys to the guild's next conference in the hope of locks being especially manufactured for them – (he gave no thought to the possibility that such locks might already exist). These locks would then secure a – far from ostentatious – chest – one replete with the qualities of *wabi sabi* – which would serve as a receptacle for his era-traversing knot.

As for the keys – the locksmith considered it important that whoever was to open the chest and find the knot ought to show his or her worthiness of being the one to discover it by first finding – through prolonged meditation as well as inspired intuitions – a means to create their own set of keys that would open the padlocks – the locksmith had already designed a mechanism whereby any opening of the chest other than by the correct opening of the padlocks would result in the knot being destroyed – thus ensuring the non-development of the *taijitu* symbology in a culture not prepared for it.

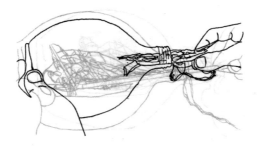

(He would later – not wishing to underestimate the keys' significance in and of themselves – use them as templates for a set of chess pieces which he had been recently commissioned to design.)

Once a chest had been acquired – one that was not too large – but neither could it be too small – the knot would need space to breathe – the locksmith booked himself a place on the Clipper that would be sailing the next day – he wished to cast the chest into the sea at a particular – prescribed place some distance to the east of the coastline of the isle of Kriti – for it was at around this juncture of the waves that – he had been informed – there flowed just the kind of temporal rift which would deposit his chest on a shore of several centuries previous.

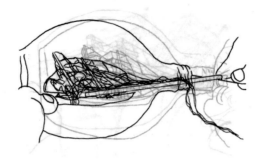

The locksmith had always loved watching the Clipper – its name was *THE ELEVATION-always-BUOYANCY* – sailing in and out of the harbour – and – while aboard ship – he thought of a fitting and final addition to the chest's interior.

He would encase the knot in a replica of the Clipper – in his cabin – also minutely mimicked – which he would then put in a bottle before placing it in the chest before casting into the sea. Of course – his replication would have to include a miniature – barely visible – copy of himself fashioning the duplicate Clipper within the cloned cabin – containing an almost inconceivable replica of the knot – and so on – incorporating – he could not resist – his self of several days earlier – walking on the felt shore – and – why not – in a whimsical touch – a tiny figure of a young – wistful mystic – praying at the sea's edge – and it was this final addition that saw the following turn of events.

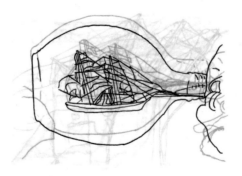

As he spent increasing amounts of time working on the ship-in-a-bottle in his cabin – his hands began to operate at greater and greater speed – almost despite himself – until – one morning when the sea was in a state of dead calm – his hands – in a near tornado of silent and serene activity – detached themselves from his body – and – still somehow continuing their work – the primary knot having already been placed in the diminutive cabin – glided across the cabin – the original one – and placed themselves into the open chest.

Far from being distressed – there was – other than the absence of his hands – no hint of severance – no blood or pain at the ends of his wrists – the locksmith saw this chain of events as being – his intensive meditative practice enabling such a view – entirely logical.

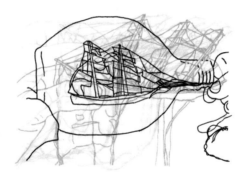

With his bare feet he managed to close all 13 locks – at which point he called for assistance in carrying the chest up on deck – they had reached the appointed coordinates for the chest's jettisoning.

On returning home – the locksmith – after an emotional farewell to the other members of the guild – set off as an itinerant mendicant – happy in the knowledge that – one day – his chest would be found – and that someone – in the past – of very special nature and calling – would use its contents to develop the very symbology that the locksmith had not only so earnestly studied – but also – in a mysterious sense – initiated.

Many years later – the locksmith – now a mendicant – after being away from his home town since the losing of his hands – an incident the causes of which had entirely escaped his recollection – decided to return – to see how the guild was progressing and to prepare himself for the end of his current cycle of existence.

Some months previously – a young man – though expressive of a kind of youth that was old beyond his years – his name was *AFFIRMATION-other-WISDOM* – on the nearby seashore adjoining this same town – was coming to the end of a protracted session of prayer – during which he had been asking the higher beings to send him an answer to the question –

'____ __ __ ____ _____ __ ____ ____?'

He had been led to this inquiry by his daily observances of the coming and going of a Clipper to the nearby harbour...